Karlaboy

by Steven Peros

SAMUEL FRENCH

FOUNDED 1830

NEW YORK HOLLYWOOD LONDON TORONTO

SAMUELFRENCH.COM

ISBN 978-0-573-69724-1   Printed in U.S.A.   #29153

IMPORTANT BILLING AND CREDIT
REQUIREMENTS

In an earlier version, ***KARLABOY*** was first presented by Love Swing Productions, in association with Hillwood Productions, Inc., at The Actors Circle Theatre, in West Hollywood, California, on October 20, 1994. It was directed by Steven Peros; the setting was by Jerry Shimer; the lighting by Chris Wasilauskas; the original music by Christopher Caliendo. The Line Producer was Jennifer Taylor Scott and the Stage Manager was Tracy Rowe. The cast was as follows:

HAROLD BACHMAN...............................H.M. Wynant
KARLA DAVEN..................................... Ellie Valleau
BILL LAUDER.................................. James McManus
TONY .... Dean Tarrolly
STUDIO BOSS.................................... Morris Beers

The ENSEMBLE (Ellen Goldwasser, Henry Lide, Lawrence Maki) portrayed: **FIRST MALE VOICE, SECOND MALE VOICE, THIRD MALE VOICE, ASSISTANT, OLGA, OLGA'S PARTNERS, PARTY GUESTS, YES MAN #1, YES MAN #2, GOWNED ACTRESS, REPORTER #1, REPORTER #2, REPORTER #3, SYDNEY BACHMAN**

THE CHARACTERS

HAROLD BACHMAN – 65, a movie director and screenwriter, retired for over 35 years. In recall, he is in his 20s.

KARLA DAVEN – 20s, a lovely actress with star quality. Karla should not be costumed or made-up to recall any one specific famous movie star.

BILL LAUDER – 30s, a journalist.

TONY – 20s-30s, a good-looking movie star-in-training.

STUDIO BOSS – 40s-60s, head of the unnamed major studio to which Harold and Karla are under contract.

ENSEMBLE OF THREE – Made up of 2 men and 1 woman. The Ensemble plays the following roles: First Male Voice, Second Male Voice, Third Male Voice, Assistant, Olga, Olga's Partners, Super Mogul, Party Guests, Yes Man #1, Yes Man #2, Gowned Actress, Reporter #1, Reporter #2, Reporter #3, Sydney Bachman, Bill's Agent

A NOTE ON CASTING

KARLABOY was written to have the role of "Harold Bachman", young and old, portrayed by one actor, very much like "Salieri" – young and old – was played by one actor in the stage version of *Amadeus* by Peter Shaffer. The effect achieved is that the audience is never viewing pure flashback. Having the older actor portray himself as a younger man in flashbacks brings an inherent melancholy as well as a sense that what we are witnessing is not objective truth, but rather viewed through the complex prism of memory. However, since some theatre companies may not find an actor who can convincingly portray both older and younger versions, permission is granted to utilize two actors in the role if deemed absolutely necessary.

Similarly, the roles beyond the first five listed above were written to be portrayed by a three-actor ensemble. This, too, helps create on stage the "life of the mind", the sense that memories, images, and faces, often jumble together, and may even repeat. Again, what we are seeing is not always pure objective truth, but Harold's own personal truth, whether he realizes it or not.

TIME AND PLACE

The action of the play takes place in 1990 in Karlaboy, a Hollywood mansion built in 1952, and, in recall, 1950-1956 in and around Hollywood, California.

The play is divided into numbered scenes, indicating a change of time or locale or mood. The action, however, is continuous and must flow from scene to scene seamlessly.

The play should be performed with one intermission.

THE SET

The main set, the sitting room of Karlaboy, as described in I:2, should be designed in such a way as to allow all its component parts – chairs, end tables, dressers, fixed props, etc. – to be utilized in the flashback scenes to other locations (Harold's pre-Karlaboy bungalow, office of Studio Boss, Oscar Party, et al). This will aid in the seamless flow from scene to scene, without having to pause for new set elements.

The main set has a staircase, as indicated in I:2. In the inaugural production, a two-level set could not be achieved, thus, the center aisle of the theatre became the de facto staircase, which allowed for staircase scenes, entrances, and exits to be played in the aisle. Similarly, when gesturing to the staircase, Harold would indicate this same aisle. This solution is recommended for any theatre or theatre company that is unable to accommodate a staircase.

The 16mm projector indicated in I:2, can also be achieved via a flickering lighting effect behind a cut-out in the rear flat, as if the projector described were contained within a projection booth or closet.

The "neon light design" indicated in II:2 was created via a simple stencil colored lighting effect. It faded up during all scenes set in Karlaboy of the past and faded out during all scenes set in the present, indicating that it is presently burnt-out.

ACT ONE

Scene One

*(We begin in darkness when suddenly perfect lighting illuminates **KARLA DAVEN**, a beautiful young actress in her twenties.)*

*(We are witnessing the final moments of her 1950 screen test. **KARLA** is confident, assured, charming.)*

*(**TWO MALE VOICES** address her from off.)*

FIRST MALE VOICE. Perfect.

SECOND MALE VOICE. Tail Slate.

*(An **ASSISTANT** rushes in and holds an upside-down movie slate in front of **KARLA**'s face.)*

ASSISTANT. Karla Daven! Screen Test! Take One!

*(The **ASSISTANT** claps the slate and exits.)*

FIRST MALE VOICE. Hold on. Keep it rolling.

KARLA. What's next, gentlemen?

SECOND MALE VOICE. We don't have to do the scene a second time, that's for sure.

*(**KARLA** smiles at the vote of approval.)*

FIRST MALE VOICE. Recite something for us.

SECOND MALE VOICE. Yeah. A little Shakespeare.

(There is laughter from the unseen voices.)

KARLA. Don't laugh. I was Desdemona up in Pasadena last Spring. "Men's natures wrangle with inferior things, though great ones are their object. For let our finger ache, and it endues our other healthful members to that sense of pain. Nay, we must – "

(An interruption from the voices.)

FIRST MALE VOICE. Great, Karla, now turn right. We want to check out your profile.

(**KARLA** *turns her formidable physique, but then playfully looks back towards the voices in the dark.*)

KARLA. How's this?

FIRST MALE VOICE. That's fine, doll, but turn your face to the right, too.

(**KARLA** *smiles, obeying the simple request.*)

SECOND MALE VOICE. *(admiringly)* What a side view.

KARLA. *(loving it)* Fresh.

SECOND MALE VOICE. Camera's heading for a run-out.

FIRST MALE VOICE. Okay. Let's wrap this up. Karla, give us a kiss, you know, right to the camera. Play a little.

(*What a show* **KARLA** *gives. In the tilt of her head, the seductiveness of her bedroom eyes, the pucker of her lips, there is enough sex appeal to set several thousand movie screens on fire.*)

KARLA. How's that? Should I do it again?

(*The voices in the dark are silent with admiration.*)

(*There are several bright flashes of light and then Blackout.*)

(*In the darkness:*)

HAROLD. Beautiful, isn't she?

BILL. Yes. She was.

Scene Two

(*Lights come up on the Main Sitting Room of Karlaboy. Present.*)

(*This is a two-story mansion built in the early 1950s. Once immaculate, it is now a bit unkempt and musty. Neat piles of newspapers and magazines can be found behind furniture and along walls, unrecycled.*)

(There is a staircase, leading to rooms above. Two men are the only occupants.)

*(**HAROLD BACHMAN**, 65, he is a white-haired, well-composed man of fierce intellect. He is wearing an elegant silk smoking jacket, white button shirt, and casually tied ascot of subtle color.)*

*(The other is – **BILL** LAUDER, 30s, intelligent, eager, recently-awoken.)*

(They sit side by side, looking out at us, having just watched the screen test. Upstage, a 16mm projector projects empty light above the heads of the audience.)

BILL. Right there. One angle. No cuts. It's like seeing the "Mona Lisa" for the first time.

HAROLD. *(dismissive)* "Mona Lisa" was a cow. Now Karla Daven – she was the golden calf.

BILL. *(still in awe)* It's so clear, isn't it?

HAROLD. It's really your first time?

BILL. Well, yeah, considering you stole the only copy before I was born.

HAROLD. *(unamused)* I told you: I didn't steal it – I saved it. It was dying in a vault from malnutrition.

BILL. I was just kidding.

HAROLD. I see. *(a beat)* Forgive me. I wasn't prepared for the subtlety of your razor wit.

BILL. That was an insult, right? I mean, just so I'm clear.

HAROLD. Nothing flies under your radar, does it, Billy old boy?

BILL. You know, as thrilled as I am to finally meet you, it's beginning to border on masochism.

HAROLD. I show you the only known print of Karla Daven's screen test and you talk about masochism?

BILL. I'm not talking about Karla right now.

HAROLD. Well someone had better – and fast.

BILL. That would be you, Mr. Bachman. I've said all I have to say.

(**HAROLD** *gestures to a display case of Karla Daven memorabilia.*)

HAROLD. You know, there isn't a single country you can go to where that one word doesn't bring about instant recognition. Karla. Posters, t-shirts, buttons – *(picks one up:)* "Karla Died For Our Sins" *(tosses it back)* A popular one for the feminist groups in the sixties. She was their martyr for every innocent virgin corrupted into a whore by a man's world.

(**HAROLD** *returns to* **BILL.**)

HAROLD. Did you know that in the Korean War, when the girls wrote to their soldiers, they used to sign off, "Love, Kisses and Tears"?

BILL. Of course I know that.

HAROLD. Right. Of course you do.

(**HAROLD** *finally notices the "on" projector and moves to turn it off.*)

BILL. You know, this isn't what I expected.

HAROLD. Sorry. I gave my cleaning lady off for two decades.

BILL. No, not Karlaboy. You. I mean, after Karla died, you never made another film. You refuse all interviews. Only a handful of photographers have managed to catch you in over thirty years.

HAROLD. I know who I am, Bill.

(**HAROLD** *turns off the projector.*)

BILL. I guess like everyone else, I wasn't sure if you were still…

HAROLD. Functioning?

BILL. In a word.

HAROLD. Parts of me are. Parts of me aren't.

BILL. Then I'll take the insults, considering the alternative.

HAROLD. What alternative is that?

BILL. I thought I was going to walk in here tonight and find you charging across the room, swinging an ice pick at me.

HAROLD. Now why would I do that?

BILL. Because my publisher sent you a copy of the book.

HAROLD. Yes. The book.

(HAROLD picks up a thick manuscript, which lies upon a nearby table.)

HAROLD. "Karla, Oh Boy! The Secret Life of Karla Daven, by Bill Lauder." Your revisionist testament that my wife was not an innocent girl corrupted by Hollywood, but rather – a shameless whore who self-destructed.

(He throws the manuscript back down on the table with a slam.)

HAROLD. Now why on Earth would I let a little thing like that bring me to violence?

BILL. *(after letting the above register)* Mr. Bachman, can I be straight with you?

HAROLD. Of course, Bill.

BILL. Well, I'm just barely getting over the shock of your call and driver and seeing that it really is Karlaboy I've been driven to. I mean, it's all a bit overwhelming.

HAROLD. That's very flattering.

BILL. Flattery aside, I'd really appreciate it if you could be straight with me.

HAROLD. You want me to be straight? Stop referring to this goddamn mausoleum as "Karlaboy." *(mimicking him cruelly)* "I've never been to *Karlaboy*" – "I can't believe I'm really in *Karlaboy*."

BILL. Fine, fine, sorry. I didn't know.

HAROLD. Well now you do.

(HAROLD rises and leans against the fireplace, upon which sits a single Academy Award®.)

HAROLD. Time's a' wastin', Bill, so I'll get right to the point: It is now one-forty a.m. Unless we come to terms, I will be dead by three-fifteen.

BILL. That line didn't play any better an hour ago on the phone.

HAROLD. Given the caliber of your own writing, I thought you'd enjoy it.

BILL. Another dig, right? Just keeping score.

HAROLD. Listen to me clearly: unless you instruct your publishers to keep those delivery trucks in their garages, Karla is going to walk down those stairs at three-fifteen a.m. and shoot me through the forehead.

*(***BILL*** looks at ***HAROLD***, then at the stairs, then back at ***HAROLD***.)*

BILL. Karla Daven?

HAROLD. Her ghost if you want to get technical.

*(***BILL*** doesn't know whether to laugh or run for the door. He chooses neither.)*

BILL. Karla Daven's ghost…is going to show up tonight?

HAROLD. Am I going to have to keep repeating things to you all night? Yes. Her ghost is not only going to show up tonight, but has shown up yearly since her death on Oscar Eve, 1953.

BILL. Here?

HAROLD. Yes – *here.* Where the hell else would it be?

*(***HAROLD*** looks up to the darkened staircase.)*

HAROLD. She just stands up there and stares at me. Like the first time…

Scene Three

*(It is 1954. ***YOUNG HAROLD*** is twenty-nine and every bit the man he is today. Only younger.)*

(His eyes are fixed on the top of the stairs.)

*(***KARLA'S GHOST*** is standing there. Nothing but darkness behind her. Wordless. Expressionless. Her gaze locked on the trembling ***HAROLD***.)*

YOUNG HAROLD. K - K - Karla?

(She says nothing.)

YOUNG HAROLD. What do you want?

(Again, no reply. No change of expression.)

YOUNG HAROLD. Answer me!

Scene Four

(Karlaboy, The Present. **HAROLD** *still has his eyes fixed on the top of the stairs.)*

BILL. Did she?

HAROLD. Not a word. Not then and not since. She stood there until six-twenty-two a.m. – how 'bout that?

BILL. How 'bout what?

HAROLD. Some biographer. That's when they dragged her carcass out of here. Six-twenty-two on the morning of the Oscars. She died at three-fifteen, they hauled her out at six-twenty-two.

BILL. Uh-huh. *(a pause)* So you just sort of…"figure" she wants to kill you tonight?

HAROLD. Oh, no, no, no. She told me she's going to kill me.

BILL. I thought she never said a word?

HAROLD. She never did, until your goddamned book showed its face here!

*(***HAROLD** *picks up the manuscript and flips to the last page.)*

HAROLD. After putting it off as long as I could, I decided to read your abomination yesterday.

Scene Five

(Karlaboy, Yesterday. **HAROLD** *reads aloud:)*

HAROLD. "Harold was absent from her flower-filled funeral. It has always been romantically believed that Harold stayed away out of unbearable grief. But in harsh reality, he stayed away because eulogies are a time for truth, and Harold couldn't stand to tell the world the truth about Karla, the wife he loved and nurtured who paid him back only with heartache. A woman who took from her husband and the world until there was no more for her to claim. And so, finally, she took something from herself. Her life."

KARLA'S GHOST. That book is a lie.

(A startled **HAROLD** *looks to the top of the stairs)*

HAROLD. It'll be on the shelves in two days.

KARLA'S GHOST. You will die if the first copy touches the first shelf.

HAROLD. There's nothing I can do!

KARLA'S GHOST. You'll think of something.

HAROLD. It's out of my control!

KARLA'S GHOST. Then you will die.

Scene Six

(Karlaboy, The Present. **HAROLD** *tosses the book back on the lamp table and cozies into his chair, taking a silver cigarette case from the drawer as he speaks.)*

HAROLD. So you see, we really have no choice in the matter. You'll just have to call up your publishers, tell them there are too many embarrassing errors, and call the whole thing off.

(Without missing a beat, **HAROLD** *holds out the cigarette case.)*

HAROLD. Cigarette?

*(***BILL** *does not respond to the offer.)*

BILL. Mr. Bachman, do I look like an idiot to you?

*(***HAROLD** *leans in, studying* **BILL**'*s face.)*

HAROLD. Just a bit. Around the eyes.

BILL. *(ignoring the dig)* This book has been in the works for three years. I've tried to meet with you for two of them, and you've had the final galleys for six weeks. Do you actually think you can just send over a limo, offer me a drink, and casually tell me that unless I get my publishers to cancel a multi-million dollar operation that's gonna start in six hours, a ghost is gonna kill you?

HAROLD. Why else would I have waited this long?!

BILL. But why kill you? I wrote the book.

HAROLD. And I was here the night she killed herself.

(BILL takes pause, realizing he's treading on sensitive ground.)

BILL. Karla Daven took her own life. Her suicide note made it clear she blamed only herself. I mean, Mr. Bachman, if she really has been haunting you all these years, I don't see why.

HAROLD. Neither do I! Regardless, she's furious about the lies you've written and unless this book is stopped, she will kill me tonight at 3:15 on the dot.

BILL. You're still not gonna let up on this ghost thing?

HAROLD. This Ghost Thing is the goddamned truth!

BILL. Well, I'm a writer, Mr. Bachman, not a medium.

HAROLD. A medium won't work. I've tried three already.

(A moment as BILL reacts to this surprising statement. Eager to hear more.)

BILL. Really?

HAROLD. *(with a nod)* Oh yes. The first time was in '56, that was after she had appeared for two consecutive years.

Scene Seven

(Karlaboy, 1956. Young HAROLD is sitting on the floor along with OLGA, a sixty-year-old medium, and her TWO PARTNERS. The foursome is sitting cross-legged, holding hands.)

HAROLD. It was obvious that she intended to create a routine, so I wanted someone here to deal with her on her third performance.

*(**OLGA** speaks, her eyes opened but dazed, entranced.)*

OLGA. Karla…Karla…Why are you not at rest?…Why are you not at peace?…Speak to us…Show us your sorrow…Show us your sorrow and leave this place…

*(**KARLA'S GHOST** appears at the top of the stairs.)*

YOUNG HAROLD. There she is! *(He turns to one of **OLGA**'s partners.)* Do you see her? At the top of the stairs!

PARTNER #1. Please, Mr. Bachman. You must let Olga continue in silence.

OLGA. What do you want, Karla?…What do you want?

*(**KARLA'S GHOST** begins to descend the stairs. **HAROLD** is frightened. He trembles, but tries not to break the link of hands.)*

OLGA. What do you want?…How can we help you?…

*(**KARLA** is now at the foot of the stairs. She is approaching **HAROLD**. He is intensely frightened.)*

OLGA. Show us what you want, Karla…

*(**KARLA** reaches her hand out towards **HAROLD**. He can stand it no longer and leaps away.)*

*(**KARLA** continues reaching forward and grabs – The Sports section of the newspaper from a pile nearby.)*

(She sits down at the foot of the stairs and begins to read the paper.)

*(Young **HAROLD** stares down at her in disbelief.)*

Scene Eight

(Karlaboy, the Present)

HAROLD. She sat there on that step and read the goddamned Sports Page until six-twenty-two in the morning. Then she disappeared.

BILL. And the others?

HAROLD. No one saw a thing. They thought I was a raving lunatic. She sat there laughing at me. The other two séances went more or less the same way.

BILL. Okay. If you can't evict Karla, why don't you just get the hell out.

(**HAROLD** *responds as if this is the strangest question he's ever been asked.*)

HAROLD. Out? Out of here? Karla doesn't haunt these walls, she haunts me.

BILL. How can you be so sure?

HAROLD. In 1972, that phone actually rang –

(*A 1970s* **SUPER MOGUL** *appears, wrapped in a plush robe and talking on his phone. Think Bob Evans or any of the "Easy Riders, Raging Bulls" crowd. He could be smoking a joint.*)

SUPER MOGUL. Isn't there any way I can get you to come? I mean, it's The Oscars, man.

HAROLD. (*addressing the mogul*) How did you get this number?

SUPER MOGUL. Don't be uptight – I get everybody's number. Whataya say? Come on – for The Oscars.

HAROLD. I don't go to Oscar Parties.

SUPER MOGUL. People will fucking flip. And it'll be good for you. Show everyone you're not a ghost.

HAROLD. You know, in my day, no one of importance had Oscar Parties.

SUPER MOGUL. (*concerned*) They didn't?

HAROLD. No. They had "Night Before" Parties.

SUPER MOGUL. (*liking the sound of this*) Night Before?

HAROLD. Oh yes. Very chic. Shows you're above it all, completely unimpressed by the establishment. (*turning to* **BILL**) So the imbecile held one.

(*exit* **SUPER MOGUL**)

HAROLD. I, of course, was there solely for the purpose of my experiment.

BILL. And?

HAROLD. She was there. She came to this idiot's pathetically unimaginative bash...just to show me she could.

BILL. Sorry to be so blunt, Mr. Bachman, but this is really a bit...difficult, do you know what I'm saying? I mean, this is really kind of, uhm...difficult. I mean, you call me up at midnight, shouting "We must talk!" into my ear, and now I find myself listening to stories about a ghost reading the sports page and you getting shot at three-fifteen. I mean, if I understand you correctly, this is no game. You're really asking me to believe all this.

HAROLD. My life is counting on it.

BILL. I wrote the truth about Karla Daven. Hard and painful as it may be – it's the truth.

HAROLD. No it's not!

BILL. Then prove it to me.

HAROLD. How?

BILL. Show me where I was wrong. Give me the interview I've wanted for two years.

HAROLD. There's no time.

BILL. There's plenty of time. *(He looks at his watch.)* It's only two.

HAROLD. It's two?

BILL. A few minutes before.

(**HAROLD** *picks up the rotary phone and holds it out to* **BILL** *pleadingly.*)

HAROLD. Please. Stop those trucks.

BILL. You'll have to tell me why. In detail.

HAROLD. I'm a private man, Bill. I made four films in my life and fewer friends. The whole publicity game was the studio's doing.

(**BILL** *picks up his briefcase and coat.*)

BILL. Look, Mr. Bachman, I've heard you out. I've given you my offer, which is very reasonable. I mean, given what hell Karla put you through, I obviously have a lot of sympathy for you. But if you won't go into the details, I'm gonna have to say goodbye right now. You can call my publishers and hash it out with them in the morning.

HAROLD. All right, goddamn you! Sit back down.

(Having gotten what he wants, BILL sits.)

HAROLD. Fire away.

BILL. Not me, Mr. Bachman. You. You read the book – tell me where I was wrong.

HAROLD. Everywhere! Take the way you claim we met. I mean, the way you tell it, she aggressively latched on to me at an Oscar party, offering sexual favors for a role in my next film. Nothing could be further from the truth.

Scene Nine

(GUESTS suddenly fill the room as we are transported to a late night Oscar Party, 1950.)

(Young HAROLD is sitting on the sidelines, trying to have a moment with his martini.)

HAROLD. It's true that I met Karla at an Oscar party the night I lost my first nomination. The loss meant nothing to me really. I was indifferent to the picture and the awards in general...

(KARLA enters, vivacious as ever in a stunning dress, is bumped by someone and lands on the arm of HAROLD's chair, nearly spilling his drink.)

KARLA. Oh, excuse me.

YOUNG HAROLD. *(indifferent)* That's all right.

(KARLA doesn't rise. She's interested.)

KARLA. How do you do, Mr. Bachman?

(**HAROLD** *gives in reluctantly and shakes her hand.*)

YOUNG HAROLD. Fine, thank you.

KARLA. I'm Karla Daven and I loved your movie.

HAROLD. Thank you.

KARLA. I really mean it. I'll tell you the truth – I liked it a lot more than the picture that won.

(He really doesn't want to be reminded, but…)

YOUNG HAROLD. Thank you.

KARLA. I mean, all that crap about it being so much more substantial than your movie. You know, sometimes you just want fluff, and as long as it's good fluff – what's wrong with that?

YOUNG HAROLD. Yes…my film was absolutely meaningless, don't you think?

KARLA. I'm sorry. I didn't mean to offend you –

YOUNG HAROLD. Offend me? Why no, Miss Whatever-your-name-is.

KARLA. It's Karla. And I happened to see you sitting here like someone who can't speak the language so I came over to help you lighten up.

YOUNG HAROLD. As I recall, you were bumped into my lap by a rather rude character actor.

KARLA. Well, I was going to come over here eventually, but –

YOUNG HAROLD. But what? Hadn't finished with the Winner's Circle? A few more laps to "accidentally" fall on prior to mine?

KARLA. You know, I should slap your face for that.

YOUNG HAROLD. Please do – this party is putting me to sleep.

KARLA. No thanks. I only slap winners. Nighty night.

(She rises, about to walk away. **HAROLD** *is impressed by her retort.)*

YOUNG HAROLD. Very nice. Would you like to take a real seat and have a real conversation?

(**KARLA**, *now a few feet away, with her back to* **HAROLD**, *is getting the "come hither" look by a* **HANDSOME MAN**, *holding an Oscar statuette.*)

(*She smiles at the man and then turns her back to him, returning to* **HAROLD**.)

KARLA. You're very strange, Harold.

YOUNG HAROLD. I'm aware of that. What is it you do, Miss Daven?

KARLA. I'm a model. I just did a screen test for the studio you're at. Rumor has it they liked it.

YOUNG HAROLD. Any particular part?

KARLA. No. They just wanted to see if I'm usable.

YOUNG HAROLD. Usable…

KARLA. "Is Karla Daven the latest fashion in cheesecake?"

YOUNG HAROLD. You're not as green as they usually come. A lot less than I was.

KARLA. But now you're wise, huh? All cynical and hardened at – how old are you anyway?

YOUNG HAROLD. I'm in that awkward age – too young for respect and too old for my mother's tit…well, almost.

KARLA. You know, I have a tough time matching-up this smart-ass with the guy who made "The Beverly Hills Affair." I mean, that picture was such a –

YOUNG HAROLD. "A frothy romantic frolic," L.A. Times. Yes, well, life doesn't always imitate art. At least that one didn't, thank God.

KARLA. So you got one that does? You know – the old "script in the drawer"?

YOUNG HAROLD. I do.

KARLA. Can I read it?

YOUNG HAROLD. It's not ready to leave my drawer.

KARLA. Then bring the girl to the script.

YOUNG HAROLD. I'll think about it. When can you come by?

KARLA. This party's a bust. How about now?

YOUNG HAROLD. Now? Be the first to leave the town's biggest Oscar bash? Together no less?! Karla, I'm beginning to like you more and more.

Scene Ten

(Harold's Pre-Karlaboy bungalow. He is fishing through a stack of scripts and paper for a copy of the script.)

YOUNG HAROLD. *(calling)* I'll be out in a minute.

(As he continues the search, he is unaware that **KARLA** *has entered and is moving closer. He finds the script and calls out:)*

YOUNG HAROLD. Here it – *(he turns and sees* **KARLA**, *lowering his voice)* …is.

(She takes the script, but keeps her eyes on **HAROLD**.*)*

KARLA. Thank you, Harold.

(She kisses **HAROLD** *on the lips. He seems a bit embarrassed, but silent. She continues kissing him.)*

YOUNG HAROLD. Karla?

KARLA. *(still kissing)* Yes…

YOUNG HAROLD. Stop Karla.

KARLA. *(continuing)* Yeah…

YOUNG HAROLD. No. I mean really stop.

*(***KARLA** *stops.)*

KARLA. What's the matter?

YOUNG HAROLD. I don't…it doesn't do anything for me.

KARLA. What…what do you mean?

(He is amused at her confusion.)

YOUNG HAROLD. What do you think I mean?

KARLA. Are you saying that you're…well, I mean… Are you queer?

YOUNG HAROLD. What if I said yes?

KARLA. I'd be shocked.

YOUNG HAROLD. Why?

KARLA. Well, you're very sexy, Harold.

YOUNG HAROLD. *(agreeing)* I am.

KARLA. "Am" what? Queer or sexy?

YOUNG HAROLD. I'd like to think both.

KARLA. So I don't do anything for you?

YOUNG HAROLD. Like the studio report indicates, you are indeed "one helluva tomato" – but still, I remain unaffected.

KARLA. So, you did know who I was tonight.

YOUNG HAROLD. Well…yes.

KARLA. "Miss Whatever-your-name-is." Your loss, Harry.

YOUNG HAROLD. Not entirely. I really want you to read this. There's a part in here you'd be ideal for.

KARLA. That's a line.

YOUNG HAROLD. I already told you, I'm not after your tomatoes. Although they are magnificent.

KARLA. Thanks…I guess.

(She begins flipping through the script.)

KARLA. What's it about?

YOUNG HAROLD. Well, the kinks haven't been worked out yet, but essentially, it's about a man fighting to maintain his integrity in the face of incredible opposing forces. Your role would be the woman by his side who thrives on his strength and commitment.

KARLA. Sort of like "The Fountainhead"?

YOUNG HAROLD. No, not quite that extreme.

*(**KARLA** impulsively takes **HAROLD** and kisses him with everything she's got. As they come out of it –)*

KARLA. Nothing, huh?

*(**HAROLD** shrugs.)*

KARLA. Damn.

(She picks up the script and taps **HAROLD** *in the chest with it.)*

KARLA. I'll read it and get back to ya.

YOUNG HAROLD. "I'll read it and get back to ya"? An Oscar-nominated director offers you a script that you didn't have to sleep with him for – something new young things on the lot wait their whole life for – and you say, "I'll read it and get back to ya"? *(a beat)* What brought a breath of clean air like you into this armpit of the Western World?

KARLA. Look, I gave it a shot 'cause I wanted to try it. Now that I tried it, I like it. So I'll keep at it until they don't want me anymore. But I mean I never expected this to go anywhere.

YOUNG HAROLD. The hell with that. I want and demand to go everywhere. None of the concessions I've made – this fluff I've been doing – is good enough. I refuse to be short-changed.

KARLA. Yeah, but sometimes you only realize you've been stiffed after you walk out of the store.

YOUNG HAROLD. I never walk out without counting my change. And I suggest you don't either, if you know what's good for you.

Scene Eleven

(Karlaboy, The Present)

HAROLD. Word got out about Karla's screen test and everyone wanted her. But I had her. The studio was not so keen about using my "script in the drawer" as her first picture. They decided for a more safe, commercial endeavor. So, we did "Girl in the Park" instead – a wonderfully weightless smash hit. *(a pause)* But that's the way we met, not the sordid calculated way you imagined. Contemptible little assumptions because we left together and I offered her a part in my film.

(BILL has no response.)

HAROLD. So? What do you have to say to that?

BILL. Well, I'd heard all the stories about you…"experimenting a little in your youth." Practically everyone seemed to back then. But all my research indicates that your bisexual lifestyle stopped when you got involved with Karla.

HAROLD. I see. For lack of evidence to the contrary, you decided that I'd "gone straight." What sort of "research" did you do? Dust all the male rectums in Hollywood for my penis prints?

BILL. Karla married you knowing this? I mean, did you continue with that lifestyle during your marriage?

HAROLD. It would put an awful wrench in your thesis, wouldn't it? "The devoted husband waiting for his heartless, whoring wife to come home."

BILL. If you're telling the truth.

HAROLD. I AM NOT LYING!

BILL. All right, all right, Jesus, calm down.

(The two men calm for a moment.)

BILL. I still don't understand how it's remained such a secret. I mean, so tight that, that –

HAROLD. That even a shameless "over-turner of rocks" like you didn't find out.

(BILL chooses not to respond to this insult.)

HAROLD. I took a hiatus. No, more like a forced retirement.

Scene Twelve

(The Office of the STUDIO BOSS. He is flanked by TWO YES MEN. YOUNG HAROLD is before them. The set-up more than smacks of an interrogation.)

STUDIO BOSS. How far are you planning to go with this queer thing, Harold?

YOUNG HAROLD. How far?

STUDIO BOSS. Yes. How far?

YOUNG HAROLD. I don't know. *(flirting)* How far would you like me to go?

STUDIO BOSS. Harold, you're good. Our very own "Boy Wonder" Bachman.

YOUNG HAROLD. For God's sake – I told you how much I hate that name.

STUDIO BOSS. And God has heard you, but He still likes it on the press releases.

(The **STUDIO BOSS** *lifts a script off the table.)*

STUDIO BOSS. Now. This script of yours. I don't like it. None of us do. It doesn't make any sense.

YES MAN #1. No sense at all.

STUDIO BOSS. It needs a lot of work.

YES MAN #2. A lot of work.

YOUNG HAROLD. What are you getting at?

STUDIO BOSS. We're not making the picture.

YOUNG HAROLD. But you agreed that after "Girl in the Park" –

STUDIO BOSS. It's depressing. And in the end, the two fruity guys become partners and dump the girl.

YOUNG HAROLD. They're friends, for Christ's sake! It's a film about the integrity that –

STUDIO BOSS. Even Hope and Crosby don't dump the girl, Harold, and they are great friends.

YES MAN #1. Great friends.

STUDIO BOSS. You're gonna do this one instead.

*(***HAROLD** *is handed a script by one of the* **YES MEN***. A much thinner script than his own personal epic. The title:)*

YOUNG HAROLD. "Love Swing"?!?

*(***HAROLD** *throws it back at the* **YES MEN***.)*

I won't do another one of these things!

STUDIO BOSS. You do them very well, Harold. If "Beverly Hills Affair" and "Girl in the Park" are any indication, the audience loves paying to see you do it. You will continue to make light –

YOUNG HAROLD. Fluffy romantic shit! I won't do it!

STUDIO BOSS. Listen, Harold, your contract is written in harder stone than the cement at Grauman's Chinese. I'm sure you also remember the moral's clause as well as our control over publicity. *(a pause)* This queer thing would be very negative for the studio and your career as a director of…how did he put it?

(Both **YES MEN** *rush to answer first.)*

BOTH YES MEN. Fluffy romantic shit.

STUDIO BOSS. Yes. Therefore, if you would rather be assigned dental hygiene films in New Jersey, I recommend that any mention of this queer thing not leave this room. Do we understand each other, Harold?

Scene Thirteen

(Karlaboy, the Present. **HAROLD** *is mixing himself a drink.)*

HAROLD. All right, perhaps my memory tends to overdramatize the past. But it was something like that and they did threaten me.

BILL. I read through all the studio memos relating to you and Karla. There was no mention of this topic.

HAROLD. Why should there be? I was married to the sexiest woman in Hollywood.

BILL. But what about the press? I've been through every fan magazine and society column. Again, no mention.

HAROLD. Well, Bill, if I was as deluded as most people in this town, I'd tell you that the press is sensitive towards homosexuals. That their liberal hearts "care" enough to respect their privacy. Unfortunately that's a crock of dog shit. The silence of the press is motivated completely out of self-interest. If the press reported about every gay – eighty goddamned percent of the Hollywood community, by my estimates – Mr. and Mrs. Front Porch would keel over and never buy another entertainment magazine or newspaper again. You see, Bill, it's bad for the news business to make gay newsworthy. They will accept adultery and drug abuse from their idols, but they will not allow them to turn on them sexually. It's the biggest slap in the face imaginable. It's just not done…at least not while they're alive. *(a beat)* But why am I telling you this? You're the sort of writer who's well aware that Heterosexuality Sells Movie Tickets. Homosexuality Sells Posthumous Biographies.

BILL. You know who buys respectable, analytical film biographies? Movie Geeks. You know who buys biographies that name each and every one of their lovers? The same movie geeks plus everyone else. I didn't create the phenomenon.

HAROLD. No. You just take advantage of it but with a carefully placed tear in your eye for the human condition.

BILL. Oh I see. You've just gone ahead and put me down in that sewer where you put everyone else, huh?

HAROLD. Everyone. Except Karla.

BILL. Don't you think I have the same respect for Karla?

HAROLD. Respect?!?

*(**HAROLD** suddenly begins to rifle through a bureau while **BILL** continues –)*

BILL. Yes. Respect. I loved Karla. I researched her life as a labor of that love.

*(**HAROLD** pulls an eight-by-ten photo out of the bureau. Holds it right up to **BILL**'s face. NOTE: We only see the photo from the rear.)*

HAROLD. And you express that love by printing this in your book?! Karla on the coroner's slab?! Her head blown wide open?!

BILL. Karla Daven's suicide has been glamorized and romanticized out of all proportion. I had to put that picture in there to smack people in the face with the pathetic grainy ugliness of her death.

HAROLD. How very philanthropic of you, Bill. I wish I could have been there when this photograph came in contact with your sweaty fingertips. I wish I could have seen that great thin-lipped, ear-to-ear smile slither across your face. I'm sure it was filled with images of "your great contribution to humanity." Or was it "humanity's contribution to your bank account"?

BILL. Very nice, Mr. Bachman. Talk like that is sure going to win me over at the grand old hour of two-twenty.

HAROLD. Two-twenty?! Bill, I need an answer! She is going to kill me tonight!

BILL. Your sweet innocent Karla Daven is planning a cold-blooded murder. Strangely inconsistent, wouldn't you say?

HAROLD. You've driven her to it! I'm telling you, she was an innocent when she came to this town! She didn't even know how to sign her own autograph, for Christ's sake!

Scene Fourteen

(Harold's Pre-Karlaboy bungalow, 1951. **KARLA** *is sitting on the floor with a stack of eight-by-ten glossies strewn before her. She signs her name to one and holds it up to* **YOUNG HAROLD.***)*

KARLA. How about this?

YOUNG HAROLD. Awful. You sign like some little girl in grammar school penmanship class. It has to have flair, uniqueness, beauty. A fan sits by the mailbox for weeks waiting for this to arrive. Waiting for something sent down to them from that high pedestal they've built for you. What comes out of that envelope cannot disappoint. Give me one.

(KARLA hands HAROLD a photo. He pauses a moment, looks at the photo, the pen in his hand. He signs it and hands it back to KARLA.)

KARLA. That's great! Let me practice.

(KARLA studies HAROLD's autograph and takes a crack at it.)

KARLA. How' this?

YOUNG HAROLD. Close. Keep trying. Give me some. I can help.

(KARLA happily hands him a stack of photos.)

YOUNG HAROLD. What are you signing?

KARLA. "Best wishes, Karla Daven"

YOUNG HAROLD. Good God No! "Love and Kisses, Karla Daven" Do you understand? From here on in.

KARLA. Yes sir.

(They each sign for a moment or two. KARLA seems to have something to talk about, but is formulating the words in her head.)

KARLA. Harold, have you ever been in love?

YOUNG HAROLD. The things that come out of your mouth.

KARLA. Have you?

YOUNG HAROLD. No.

KARLA. Never? Not even close?

YOUNG HAROLD. I've been infatuated. I've been in lust. I've been an idiot. But, no, I've never been in love. Have you? What is it exactly?

KARLA. Don't ask me. The last time I was really in love for sure, I was still wearing braces. *(a beat)* I just...well, I'm wondering, if you've never been in love with anyone, how do you know you're...well, you know.

YOUNG HAROLD. Am I really your first contact with a being from outer space?

(KARLA glares at him. Clearly, she won't let him avoid answering.)

YOUNG HAROLD. I suppose I've never been able to define love as anything more than gratitude for being loved. It's true that I haven't had a love life, but I have had a sex life. In that life, my preference has been men. Does that answer your question?

KARLA. You don't have to be so cold about it. I'm asking because I care. I mean, you talk a hell of a lot, Harold, but you never let people get past a certain gate with you. Know what I mean?

YOUNG HAROLD. I don't know that you'd find what's beyond that gate so interesting.

*(**HAROLD** is uncomfortable with this tack and decides to change course.)*

Enough about me. Doesn't Karla Daven have any stories that are best told in the dark?

KARLA. Sure. I had bad things happen to me.

YOUNG HAROLD. Like what? Losing out on Prom Queen.

KARLA. No...I was the Prom Queen.

YOUNG HAROLD. Of course you were.

KARLA. Hey, you think it wasn't hard just getting here? You try growing up in the sticks and telling people you want to be an actress. You think I got encouragement? "Your Great Aunt – God-rest-'er-soul – was a Nurse. Your Grandmother – may-she-rest-in-peace – worked a farm until she dropped, and you, Karla, you want to be an actress?!" I had to climb over a lot of dead bodies getting to this town.

YOUNG HAROLD. I'm sorry. It's just that condescension is an unavoidable part of my nature.

KARLA. Like I haven't noticed. Just remember: not all of us were lucky enough to have a famous actor for a father.

YOUNG HAROLD. Ah, yes, Sydney Bachman. I'm really sorry you never got to meet him, Karla. He really was the best drunken, philandering, child-hating, lovable dear-old-Dad any boy could ask for.

KARLA. Harold, I'm sorry.

YOUNG HAROLD. Oh, it's no trauma, believe me. My father was the perfect, grandfatherly character actor to the world. Quick with wise advice from behind that pipe, but he had no clue off the screen with his own blood.

(**HAROLD** *has a thought and goes to a bureau. He rifles through drawers, looking for something.*)

YOUNG HAROLD. The only place I found a father was in the movies, when he did the "Mr. Foster" pictures. Ah!

(**HAROLD** *has found what he is looking for – an eight-by-ten publicity photo.*)

YOUNG HAROLD. Each picture was a perfect, seventy-five minute, black-and-white foray into the family life he could never show us in the real Technicolor world.

(**HAROLD** *slaps the photograph.*)

YOUNG HAROLD. "Mr. Foster on Four Wheels." The most meaningless of them all. And my favorite. *(as he puts the photo away)* What about you?

KARLA. What about me what?

YOUNG HAROLD. Who are the men in your life?

KARLA. I told you – I never had any. Not for real.

YOUNG HAROLD. Not even since you've been here?

KARLA. Haven't you heard, genius? I have every American male wishing he could sleep with me.

YOUNG HAROLD. Oh you do, do you?

KARLA. You know I do. I see it in their eyes. Not just in the street, but right through the lens. I've heard some actresses are uncomfortable with the camera, but not me. It's not some mechanical monster to me. It's like…some sort of funnel to pour myself through. I know that sounds silly, but that's what it feels like every time you say "Action." I softly bite my lower lip – half a second, it's there and gone – and men fifty rows back feel a tremble in their body. *(a beat)* You talk about "the real Technicolor world"…I don't know…sometimes I wonder if I could ever impress a man in the real world the way I do on that screen.

YOUNG HAROLD. You've impressed me.

KARLA. I'm just looking for it to be right, that's all. When the man is looking at me, not some pin-up poster, all perfectly lit and touched up. *(a pause)* I know this sounds crazy, but I want a man to fall in love with everything that's ugly about me; then I'll know he's the right one. You know what I mean?

Scene Fifteen

(Karlaboy, the Present)

HAROLD. She was an amazing creature. Incredibly…god-damned…self aware…Bill?

BILL. Yeah. I'm listening.

HAROLD. Don't you see? More than any woman I've ever known, Karla was a lady. A decent, supportive, beautiful woman.

BILL. No disrespect, Mr. Bachman, but I went back to that small town of hers. You should hear the stories they tell.

HAROLD. I know what sort of stories they tell.

BILL. She may not have had a boyfriend back there…but she did have twenty.

(**HAROLD** *suddenly slaps* **BILL.** *He doesn't know how to respond.*)

HAROLD. You're in Karla's home. My dead wife's home. Remember that.

BILL. Sorry.

HAROLD. I know what sort of stories they told you. A young woman's natural sexual awakening re-told as depraved nymphomania. A town bitter over the "prom queen turned movie star" who never returned to cut the ribbon on the new bakery. Small town stories from even smaller minds. *(a beat)* But then her death finally brought cameras and attention into their desperate lives. Well, thanks to you, they've made Karla pay for escaping and never looking back.

BILL. That's not fair.

HAROLD. I'm sure you and your expense account were perfectly willing to oblige each and every one of them.

BILL. They were free to answer my questions any way they pleased.

HAROLD. How did you phrase those questions? Did you ask how high she wore her skirts as you ordered them another beer? Did you ask how much she flirted with the boys as you insisted that they have dessert with their lobster dinner?

BILL. You still think you have me all figured out, don't you?

HAROLD. Just about.

BILL. Well, that makes one of us, 'cause I'm still in the dark. I mean, if all you say is true I don't see how this marriage of yours could have happened.

HAROLD. Neither could I...but it happened all the same.

Scene Sixteen

(The office of the **STUDIO BOSS**. **YOUNG HAROLD** *barges into a meeting holding a copy of "Variety.")*

YOUNG HAROLD. What is this lunacy?!

STUDIO BOSS. Harold, we're in the middle of something here.

YOUNG HAROLD. *(reading)* "Our sources tell us that the newest and steamiest romantic couple on the back lot is none other than Boy Wonder Harold Bachman and his luscious leading lady, the untamable Karla Daven. Wedding Bells have been discussed." *(He looks up.)* What is this all about? Who okayed this?

STUDIO BOSS. We did, Harold. It's good for both your images.

YOUNG HAROLD. Screw our images – it's a lie!

STUDIO BOSS. What are you getting so angry about, huh? It's just a little fun harmless gossip for the press.

YOUNG HAROLD. Fun and harmless for who? You? This is not what's happening in my life and I won't have you saying it is!

STUDIO BOSS. Relax, Harold, willya? Did anyone say you couldn't keep doing whatever it is – God forbid – you're doing with whoever you're doing it with currently? All we're asking you to do is ride this thing out for a while.

YOUNG HAROLD. I will not!

STUDIO BOSS. We've been taking a second look at that script of yours, Harold. You know, The Fountainhead thing.

YOUNG HAROLD. It's not like "The Fount –

STUDIO BOSS. All I'm saying is that it might have some possibilities.

(**HAROLD** *does not respond.*)

STUDIO BOSS. Take it easy, Harold. It's not like we're asking you to marry her or anything.

Scene Seventeen

(*Karlaboy, the Present*)

HAROLD. And you know something? They weren't. *(as if just realizing it)* They weren't asking that at all.

BILL. But then how –

HAROLD. *(interrupting)* Quiet. You'll find out soon enough. *(a beat)* Shortly after that, I was up for my second nomination.

(*A* **GOWNED ACTRESS** *appears, envelope in hand.*)

GOWNED ACTRESS. And the winner is... *(She opens envelope.)* Not Harold Bachman!

(*Echoing sounds of applause can be heard. As if from a distant memory that won't let go.*)

Scene Eighteen

*(**HAROLD**'s Pre-Karlaboy bungalow. Dark. Someone is knocking.)*

KARLA. *(off)* Harold? Are you in there?

YOUNG HAROLD. It's open.

*(**KARLA** enters, turns on a light and gets an eyeful. **HAROLD** has trashed his bungalow. By the looks, sound, and smell of him, **HAROLD** is clearly drunk. He is sitting on the floor, holding a nearly empty bottle of booze. In the middle of the wreckage.)*

KARLA. Oh my God. What did you do?

YOUNG HAROLD. Redecorating.

KARLA. Everyone was looking for you at Sam's party. You ducked out to do this?

YOUNG HAROLD. I can't sit around smiling and making small talk with the bastards who took it away from me – again.

KARLA. Oh, Harold, honey…

YOUNG HAROLD. Well, screw 'em! I got a lot of pictures to go yet.

KARLA. *(re-assuring)* You do.

YOUNG HAROLD. A lotta more pictures with "Delectable Daven." Picture after picture after picture…

KARLA. That's right.

YOUNG HAROLD. *(mumbling to himself)* Can't beat 'em join 'em…

KARLA. What's that?

YOUNG HAROLD. *(very loud now:)* If you can't beat 'em, join 'em! *(normal volume:)* You wanna get married?

KARLA. Harold, you're drunk.

YOUNG HAROLD. Come on. We never fight. We don't even disagree. We're always together, on and off the set. Let's get married.

KARLA. I always wanted to marry a gay man.

YOUNG HAROLD. Come on. It'll be fun. Enough of this rumor crap – let's be a hot Hollywood couple. We'll even stage fights, you know, in restaurants and things. You can throw wine in my face! It doesn't have to be permanent or anything. We'll play a little joke for a while. Then we'll part amicably and you can marry a real man.

KARLA. Don't say –

YOUNG HAROLD. *(almost desperately)* Please?

KARLA. Oh God. You're serious.

YOUNG HAROLD. You said yourself that you're not interested in anyone now. Can't you keep me company 'til you find someone?

KARLA. If you still want to when you're sober...I'll think about it.

YOUNG HAROLD. Are you serious? Don't kid me.

KARLA. Yes. I'm serious.

(**HAROLD** *embraces* **KARLA,** *crying tears of joy.*)

YOUNG HAROLD. I don't think my maid will ever clean this up. We'll have to get another place. Hey! Let's get a mansion! One of those big monsters! We have enough money to – screw it! Let's get the studio to pay for it. When we break it off, we'll sell it and split the studio's money! God, I'm a genius when I'm drunk.

KARLA. You really want this?

YOUNG HAROLD. *(intensely)* Yes.

(She takes a long moment to study his face.)

KARLA. Okay.

YOUNG HAROLD. *(shocked)* Okay?

KARLA. Okay.

YOUNG HAROLD. *(a pause, then:)* Why?

KARLA. Because, you idiot, marriage isn't just about sex. It's about respect and...and being who you are. To everyone else, I'm the bad daughter, the fickle girlfriend, and now the movie sex queen. *(a beat)* You let me be me, Harold.

YOUNG HAROLD. No one defines you but you. We all say other people shoe-horn us into roles, but we're really the ones who do it to ourselves.

KARLA. Hey, look, the studio made Karla and she sells tickets. It's not like that's the way people will really think I was.

YOUNG HAROLD. It's the movies you were in that will be the history lesson. After all, you've made no close friends, besides me, to vouch for "the real Karla Daven."

KARLA. Well, then, that'll be one of your jobs as my husband. To keep the balance of real and make believe in my life. I dub thee: Keeper of The Truth.

YOUNG HAROLD. I'll wear the title proudly, my lady. You're not going to regret this, Karla. I promise you.

*(A now fuzzy-headed **HAROLD**, lies his head down on her lap, and quickly drifts off.)*

HAROLD. As I lay there…my consciousness blissfully drifting away…I could swear I heard Karla say something to me. Three words that she would only have dared to whisper…because she thought I couldn't hear…

KARLA. *(softly)* I love you.

(The lights fade to darkness.)

End of Act One

ACT TWO

Scene One

(The front doors of Karlaboy, early 1950's. The press-attended ribbon-cutting for "Karlaboy" – the mansion built by the studio for **KARLA** *and* **HAROLD**.*)*

(Along with the press, **KARLA**, *Young* **HAROLD**, *and the* **STUDIO BOSS** *are present.)*

NEWSREEL REPORTER 1. Between them, they've had three hit films, two Oscar nominations and one extended honeymoon...

NEWSREEL REPORTER 2. Karla Daven and Boy Wonder Bachman returned from their European honeymoon to begin work on their third film together, "How About Darling?"...

NEWSREEL REPORTER 3. Even while they cruised the Riviera, their multi-million dollar Hollywood haven was fast on its way to completion.

*(***KARLA** *and* **YOUNG HAROLD** *are on the steps in front of their front door.* **KARLA** *carries the show, especially given* **HAROLD**'s *obvious discomfort with the event.)*

KARLA. Hey you cuties, thanks for showing up for a little old thing like the ribbon cutting on our cozy little mansion, Karlaboy.

(Applause and cheers from the crowd. Flash bulbs pop mercilessly.)

KARLA. Ah, you can't fool me. All you have to do is put out some snacks, pour a little booze, and you guys would show up for anything!

*(***KARLA** *and* **HAROLD** *each grab one loop of the over-sized prop scissors and try to cut the ribbon.)*

KARLA. Make yourself at home!

REPORTER #1. How about, Mr. Bachman?

REPORTER #2. Yeah, what's the Boy Wonder got to say?

YOUNG HAROLD. This is our home. We intend to have a happy life here. I hope you will all grant us the serenity to pursue that happiness.

(*The* STUDIO BOSS *steps forward to take up the gauntlet of merriment that* HAROLD *has just thrown into the mud.*)

STUDIO BOSS. Come on, folks. Music! Food! Booze! And it's all on me! (*with a wink*) For another hour anyway, then I take it all back to the studio!

(*Laughter all around, except, of course, from* HAROLD.)

Scene Two

(*Inside Karlaboy, 1952.* HAROLD *at the bar, fixing a drink.*)

KARLA. It's over. Okay?

YOUNG HAROLD. Look, Karla, all that phony crap may be just dandy for parties and premieres, but we live here. Do they have to follow us into our only private sanctum, for Christ's sake?!

KARLA. You know, it's very easy for you to want privacy. I'm an actress – in case you haven't noticed – and I need them to keep up my image.

YOUNG HAROLD. An image that's a lie.

KARLA. What do you want? For me to be my real self for them? A girl who's idea of the perfect Saturday night is staying home and playing chess with her gay husband?

YOUNG HAROLD. It makes no difference what you say or do. Those cameras and pens do what they want; and they're not selective either. Sure, they capture your walk down the red carpet. But they also capture every new wrinkle, every blemish, your complete disintegration!

(HAROLD takes his drink and walks about the new environment. Examining the contents for the first time.)

YOUNG HAROLD. The natives in the jungle were right: every time they take a picture, they're stealing another piece of your soul. Pieces that they keep in a dusty file folder. And when they get the last piece of your soul, Karla, the very last piece – you drop dead. Then they open up that folder and use all the pieces they've stolen for your goddamned obituary. *(a pause)* Except it all comes out in the wrong order, in the wrong... shape. Believe me, when my father died, I hardly recognized the saint they all wrote about.

KARLA. I thought this is what you wanted. It was you, you know, who talked about scenes in restaurants. Yet every time there's a camera, you run for cover. You don't want anyone to write bullshit about you, but when they ask for your own words, you hide. *(frustrated)* I mean, what do you want, Harold?!

YOUNG HAROLD. I want them to stop calling my home "Karlaboy" for starters!

KARLA. It's not your home, it's the studio's.

YOUNG HAROLD. I hate it! "Boy!" "Karla-Boy!" Pickford and Fairbanks got "Pickfair." Daven and Bachman get "Karlaboy"! I want to throw up!

KARLA. Not on this rug, Harold. We have to pay for anything we damage.

(HAROLD pours the remainder of his iceless drink onto the carpet.)

YOUNG HAROLD. That did not make me feel one bit better.

(KARLA takes a seat in the chair that HAROLD will occupy in his later scenes with BILL.)

KARLA. Next time, pee on it.

(As YOUNG HAROLD pulls down his zipper –)

KARLA. Hey! Come here and sit down.

(HAROLD recants and sits at her feet, putting his head on her lap.)

KARLA. You know, someone in this room once said that no one defines you but you.

YOUNG HAROLD. Officer, I was drunk at the time.

KARLA. Sure they own this place, but we can do what we want with it. So they're running you with this contract, but there's just one picture left on it. After that, you can do what you want with your career. With your life, for that matter. You can finally get that "script in the drawer" up on the screen.

YOUNG HAROLD. It just needs a little more tinkering. Stories of personal integrity aren't the easiest things to –

KARLA. So you'll tinker. Hey, no one's going stronger than you. "How About Darling" is going to be your best so far, and it's not just me saying that.

YOUNG HAROLD. I knew there was a reason I married you.

KARLA. And stop letting the goddamned press get to you. Between your own career and your father's, you've been in the movies all your life. You should know it comes with the territory.

YOUNG HAROLD. A lifetime in movies, a year with you, and five minutes in this elephant.

KARLA. Elephant? I like it.

YOUNG HAROLD. It's all right, I guess. Vulgar yet Tasteless.

(**HAROLD** *points to a neon light design on the wall.*)

YOUNG HAROLD. Who picked out that neon thing?

KARLA. Don't you like it? I think it's wild.

(**KARLA** *rises and stands beneath the neon design. Both she and the design glow magically.*)

KARLA. The decorator said it's the newest thing. And it'll never burn out.

Scene Three

(As the light changes to the Present, the neon light design returns to its burnt-out status. KARLA remains beneath it. HAROLD stares at her.)

BILL. Mr. Bachman?

(KARLA vanishes.)

BILL. Mr. Bachman?

HAROLD. Yes, I'm sorry.

BILL. I hate to disagree with you about what Karla liked to do on a Saturday night, but I have reports from many sources – co-stars, columnists, restaurant owners – that Karla was seen around town, trying to be discreet with many different lovers while she was married to you.

(HAROLD does not respond. He crosses to BILL. Comes within a few feet of him. BILL tenses, worried that he has crossed a line again. Finally –)

HAROLD. Can I get you a drink?

BILL. For a man who's got a ghost after him, you sure seem to be taking your time.

HAROLD. I'm goddamn petrified! Now tell me your goddamn drink!

BILL. Gin and Tonic!

HAROLD. Fine! *(as he walks off)* You're right. Karla did have affairs...

Scene Four

(Karlaboy, 1952. TONY, shirtless, well-muscled leading man type, comes thudding down the stairs with KARLA on his back piggy-back style. He puts her down and begins to kiss her all over.)

KARLA. Let's not get started again, Tony. He's coming back tonight.

TONY. It's three-thirty in the afternoon.

KARLA. That's close enough.

(TONY *continues to kiss her.*)

TONY. I don't think so.

(*She manages to create some distance.*)

TONY. Are you in love with him?

KARLA. This has got nothing to do with love, Tony. I told you that when we started all this.

TONY. It doesn't change how I feel about you.

KARLA. Look. You're incredibly sexy and a lot of fun on our "intimate afternoons"…but it'll never be more than that.

TONY. Why?

KARLA. Because I love Harold.

TONY. I don't know. There must be something…missing.

KARLA. Never mind about my life with Harold. You're in an entirely separate world. The two do not cross.

TONY. Is that what you tell yourself?

KARLA. You don't need to know what I tell myself.

TONY. I'm surprised you two ever got married. I remember when Harold was trying to come out from behind his old man's shadow –

KARLA. How did it eventually happen?

TONY. Simple: the old man told the studio he'd take a cut in salary if they let Harold write of one of the "Mr. Foster" pictures.

KARLA. "Mr. Foster on Four Wheels"?

TONY. Yeah, that's it. The car one. Turned out to be a big hit. The old man got Harold in the door and then keeled over right when the picture was finished. Anyway, my point is, back then, people were pretty sure which way the wind blew as far as Harold's sexual preference, which I'm sure you've been told. What did it take for you two to…straighten things out?

KARLA. You just don't get it, do you? There's a gate, Tony, and you're not allowed inside it. It's that simple. What we do here is just about bodies, nothing else. I use yours, you use mine. Period. It's the only thing I insisted on when we started this, remember? You liked the idea and said you could deal with my terms. If the terms have changed for you, I'll have to find someone else.

TONY. My God. Listen to you. You're exactly like him. "The Bride of Bachmanstein."

KARLA. If you knew Harold so well, how come you don't see much of each other any more?

TONY. Does he see much of anyone? Harold's got no personal connections to anyone but himself…and you, I suppose, though you won't talk about it. He's in his own fucking world with an agenda that only he knows about. Even then, he was always talking, talking, talking, but nothing he ever said had any real effect on his actions. If you've been with him this long, I'm sure you know what I mean.

(KARLA has no response.)

TONY. Hey, look. The terms haven't changed. I'm still your body to use, your body to make love to – but not to love – and your body with no mouth. There will be no more sounds from these lips that aren't completely meaningless.

(KARLA turns to him, realizing how harsh she's been.)

KARLA. Wait here a minute, okay?

TONY. I'm not going anywhere.

(KARLA disappears up the stairs.)

(TONY wanders the area. He takes a cigarette from a silver case and looks for a lighter. He finds a lighter next to a darkened archway. As he ignites the lighter, he casts a glow on a figure standing in the dark – **YOUNG HAROLD.***)*

TONY. Harold – Jesus Christ!

YOUNG HAROLD. One and the same.

TONY. You've been here…

YOUNG HAROLD. This whole time? Yes. *(after a moment or two)* It's amazing the stories we tell. How we choose to recount the past for others. You felt no hesitancy telling Karla about my way of life, yet you carefully omitted your own first hand experience on the subject.

TONY. I'm sorry, Harold.

YOUNG HAROLD. A former lover apologizes for his bisexuality after being caught in an affair with the man's wife. How sophisticated. Practically one for the Noel Coward book of Butt-Fucking Etiquette.

TONY. And what about you, Harold?

YOUNG HAROLD. What about me?

TONY. Well here you are – Married. You don't come into the clubs anymore. The word's out that you turn down every pick-up that comes-on to you. That was never the Harold Bachman I knew in the old days. Did Karla change things for you?…or have they changed?

YOUNG HAROLD. How the hell do you suppose you have the right to ask me that? Do you know where we are?

TONY. Do you? Karla just rode me piggy-back down your staircase. Most "husbands" would find the closest gun. You just stood there.

YOUNG HAROLD. Have no doubt that I'll destroy you for what I found here today.

TONY. *(amused)* You'll "destroy me"? And how would you go about that, Boy Wonder?

YOUNG HAROLD. Let's start with your dirty little secrets of days gone by.

TONY. You'd really stoop that low?

YOUNG HAROLD. You'd be amazed.

TONY. And what if I told the same stories about you, Harold?

YOUNG HAROLD. I wish to God someone would. *(a pause)* But, unfortunately, who will they believe? The Nobody? The Bachelor Actor? Or the Famous Director married to The Sexiest Woman in Hollywood?

*(Just then, **KARLA** comes trotting down the stairs.)*

KARLA. I bought this lotion in Paris when Harold and I –

YOUNG HAROLD. Ah, Karla.

(KARLA stops dead in her tracks at the sight and sound of HAROLD.)

YOUNG HAROLD. Have you met my old friend Tony? Silly me, of course you have. He was just leaving. Any objection, love?

KARLA. No.

TONY. Karla –

KARLA. Goodbye, Tony.

(TONY stares at the two of them, bowled over.)

YOUNG HAROLD. *(to TONY)* Your line is, "Goodbye."

TONY. So this is the way it is with you two.

YOUNG HAROLD. Yes, well, now that we've established that, I think it's time for you to go. I mean, now that you've made sexual conquests with both occupants of this home and been suitably screwed in return.

KARLA. What the hell does that mean?

YOUNG HAROLD. It's a private joke between Tony and me.

TONY. Why private, Harold? Come on with those "dirty little secrets of days gone by."

(HAROLD remains silent.)

TONY. I will then. You see, Karla, what you and I were doing on a "bodies only" basis, Harold and I did three years ago. Well, with some minor alterations, of course. *(He points at HAROLD.)* That man and I made love. At least I thought it was love. But for him it was just sex. Just like you, Karla, except Harold wasn't as shamelessly direct about it.

KARLA. You slept with me to get even with Harold, didn't you? You didn't feel anything at all.

TONY. Oh no, you're not gonna get off the hook that easy – I felt everything for you. I can feel love for a woman, man, black, Chinese, any make and model on the planet. It's difficult enough to find someone to love; I never felt the need to limit my options.

KARLA. *(incredulous)* Are you saying that this whole thing is a coincidence??

TONY. Being married to Harold is what first drew me in... but it's not why I fell in love with you.

*(***TONY*** *turns back to* **HAROLD.***)*

TONY. That's one of the things I'm pretty naked about, isn't it, Harold: when I'm in love. *(a pause)* But you don't know how to move from sex to love, do you? Or from love to sex, for that matter. *(to* **KARLA***)* I wonder which foot he started on with you, Karla. I wonder which foot he'll end up on...if either.

(There is a moment or two of silence in the room. Finally –)

TONY. I'm making an ass of myself.

(He grabs his shirt and walks toward the door. Before going he turns back to **KARLA***.)*

TONY. I really am sorry.

(He leaves. The sound of Karlaboy's door closing is all we hear. Then silence for a few moments.)

YOUNG HAROLD. I'm sorry, Karla.

KARLA. I'm caught and you're sorry?

YOUNG HAROLD. Caught doing what? Being human? Keeping to the agreement we made?

KARLA. I agreed to be honest.

YOUNG HAROLD. Do you want to leave me?

KARLA. I said I'd leave you when I fell in love with someone. That's why I kept Tony a secret. It wasn't love, but...I didn't know how you'd handle it.

YOUNG HAROLD. Maybe we shouldn't take this so seriously. After all, all we're talking about is physical gratification. There's nothing wrong with that, is there? You can continue with someone else, if you like. It's just Tony in particular I object to. *(a pause)* I mean, it's not like you're the only one in this relationship who needs to find sexual stimulation in someone else's arms. I've done the same thing. It's nothing.

KARLA. *(gently)* Do you still think I can't see through you when you're lying?

YOUNG HAROLD. Is it that obvious?

(She nods.)

KARLA. Did you leave Tony because he was falling in love with you?

YOUNG HAROLD. I don't know. Maybe. *(a pause)* Sometimes I think I left because…I was falling in love with him.

*(After a few moments, **BILL** interjects, which signals the lighting change back to the Present.)*

Scene Five

(Karlaboy, the Present)

BILL. Whatever happened to this Tony?

HAROLD. Nothing at all. One of the studios had signed him and was going to build him up slowly. But after I planted just the right whispers in just the right ears, there was no chance for him. I think I saw him once in a cheap Spaghetti Western shot in Yugoslavia. You know, the kind where eight different international "never-was" types are speaking eight different languages and then they dub it accordingly. It must be awful – you know what's coming out of your mouth, but you have no clue what the hell anyone else is saying. But then, even Tony has to eat…I suppose.

BILL. So your little image tonight of "The Last Decent Man" doesn't entirely hold up, does it?

HAROLD. Everyone is driven to madness…every now and then.

BILL. I don't think it's that simple. The more you talk, the more the inconsistencies keep popping up.

HAROLD. Like what?

BILL. Like your father. He put himself on the line for you. I mean, he may have been lousy, but he tried to make things up to you towards the end. You conveniently leave that part out when you talk about him.

HAROLD. We all doctor our history a little to re-invent ourselves. Create bigger and badder wolves in our past to elicit sympathy votes. The truth is that most of the time he was a drunken, miserable man who never knew how to express love to his family...so he handed out favors. But he was never the malicious man I portray him as. Just sad really.

BILL. Have you been doctoring any other history for your own benefit tonight?

HAROLD. I don't need to doctor my history – my history doctors me. Just look at the movies I made. Complete garbage, like I always said – except for her.

BILL. Hold on there, Mr. Bachman, I've watched them hundreds of times, practically frame by frame, and even under the microscope, they're still so...alive.

HAROLD. *(not persuaded)* I was under contract. I had to do them. Once I sat down to Day One on each of them, I pretended to love them, from first to last page of the script. *(a pause)* I guess if you build something on the pretense of love rather than the real thing...you'll be found out sooner or later.

BILL. I'll give you this much: you brought out the magic in Karla. No one can take that away from you. Not even you.

HAROLD. I brought out the magic in Karla because she brought out the magic in me. I loved to look at her. To watch her move. Her eyes. The way she spoke. Such effortless commitment to each and every word. The way she communicated to the camera in some sort of coded language that could only be deciphered when you were sitting out there in the dark. Karla did more than make love to the camera – others were able to do that – Karla let it make love to her. *(a pause)* I think there, in our movies, was the only place we found some sort of ground to stand on. Together. The only place we could make sense out of what we'd done. In the movies.

Scene Six

(Karlaboy, 1952. **KARLA** *walks up to* **YOUNG HAROLD** *and gives him a tremendous slap in the face.)*

KARLA. I may have been born and raised in the mountains, Mr. Cornpepper, but I am not a mountain girl.

YOUNG HAROLD. Are you or aren't you, Karla?

KARLA. I'm not.

YOUNG HAROLD. Are you positive?

KARLA. She's not. If Josie says she's not a mountain girl, then I believe her.

YOUNG HAROLD. Telling Cornpepper is one thing, but do you mean it?

KARLA. Yes.

YOUNG HAROLD. And what do you see in his eyes? What do you want to see?

KARLA. I don't know.

YOUNG HAROLD. Exactly! That's the part that you've been missing: the not-knowing. There's nothing wrong with a character not knowing what they want. Forget about all these "movie" characters who always have a clear sense of purpose. Josie's a character I shipped in from the real world.

KARLA. I like that.

YOUNG HAROLD. If we know what everybody in a movie really wants in the first fifteen minutes, well, then, forget the popcorn, let's go home. You're the mystery. You are their reason to stay.

(He strokes her cheek gently, admiringly.)

You always have been.

(She kisses his hand as it passes her lips. He stares at her as she does this. Their eyes are locked on each other. After a moment, he abruptly moves away from her.)

YOUNG HAROLD. Now, what was the other scene you had questions about?

KARLA. Oh. The scene where they're dancing and fighting.

YOUNG HAROLD. What about it?

KARLA. Well, Jack is so clumsy with the steps, I can't figure out how it's supposed to work.

YOUNG HAROLD. We'll go over it tomorrow with the choreographer.

KARLA. You do it with me. *(in character:)* Mr. Cornpepper, I don't remember the last time I danced like this.

YOUNG HAROLD. This is silly, Karla. I don't know the lines.

KARLA. I see your lips moving along out of the corner of my eye every time we rehearse.

YOUNG HAROLD. All right, all right, fine. Start again.

(Tango music, or some other sophisticated dance music from the era, kicks in.)

KARLA. Mr. Cornpepper, I don't remember the last time I danced like this.

YOUNG HAROLD. Then why do you do it so well?

KARLA. Pardon me?

YOUNG HAROLD. I said, if you haven't danced in so long, how come you do it so well? Why, in fact, are you leading?

KARLA. Just what are you getting at, Mr. Cornpepper?

YOUNG HAROLD. That you've danced often. That you've danced recently. That you've danced with other men. Probably as recently as last night.

*(**KARLA** "breaks character" and steps away. The dance music is abruptly stopped.)*

KARLA. See, Harold, here's where I don't get it – I'd be pissed off if –

*(**HAROLD** takes her back in the dancer's embrace.)*

YOUNG HAROLD. No. Don't stop and you'll see what I mean. The point is that Josie has been dancing with other men.

KARLA. But he doesn't know that she –

YOUNG HAROLD. Just keep dancing and you'll see. Come on.

KARLA. *(back in character)* You can believe what you want, Mr. Cornpepper, but I want you to know that you've hurt my feelings. Deeply. By these unfounded accusations.

YOUNG HAROLD. Like how many other men have hurt your feelings?

KARLA. Mr. Cornpepper, I won't stand another minute of your –

YOUNG HAROLD. Josie, I don't care who else you dance with or who else you kiss. I just care that you're there for me when I need to dance with you...when I need to kiss you. And I care that when you speak to me, you speak the truth.

KARLA. You want to know the truth, Mr. Cornpepper.

YOUNG HAROLD. Yes.

KARLA. I want to know your first name.

YOUNG HAROLD. I'm sorry, Josie. I told you from the start – The Agency forbids us from divulging our real names when we're on a mission. Cornpepper isn't even my real last name.

KARLA. So give me a fake first name.

YOUNG HAROLD. What name would you like to call me?

KARLA. How about "Darling"?

(They stare at each other as they dance and, after a moment, begin to kiss as part of the scene.)

(In the middle of the kiss – the dance music abruptly stops as **YOUNG HAROLD** *turns away, looking at* **BILL.**)

YOUNG HAROLD. What time is it?

Scene Seven

(Karlaboy, Present)

BILL. *(lost in the scene)* I love that scene.

HAROLD. I said what time is it?!

*(**BILL** snaps out of it and looks at his watch.)*

BILL. It's not three yet. It's a quarter of.

HAROLD. I need an answer!

BILL. I can't give you one yet.

HAROLD. Why the hell not?! I've explained where you were wrong. What the hell else do you need refuted?!

BILL. Your own damn words!

HAROLD. What do you mean?

BILL. The foothold of my take on Karla all started when I read your statement to the police after her death.

HAROLD. I, uh…it was such a long…

BILL. It's in my fucking book! You went on and on about how unstable she was. How depressed she'd gotten over the last few months of her life. How her wild life style tore your lives apart. You think I made this stuff up?! You've got to tell me about that part of her life too. I read and re-read that statement. Dissected every word you used. It's a fucking testimonial to a born wild-woman who finally dove right off the cliff. Your description of that last night leaves little to the imagination…

Scene Eight

(Karlaboy, 1953. **KARLA** *is pacing, absorbed in thought.* **HAROLD** *is at the bar, pouring himself a stiff drink. From his manner, it is clear he's had quite a few drinks this night.)*

YOUNG HAROLD. How about it, darling? I can't drink this bottle by myself. You have to help a bit.

KARLA. I'm too damn nervous.

YOUNG HAROLD. Tomorrow our names will be read twice. First, for their respective nominations, then as the winners. This is fate. This will be. Do you understand?

KARLA. What's happening to me, Harold? I don't know who I am anymore, what I want. I'm terrified about tomorrow night. Terrified that I'll finally get just what I want and I won't know what to do next except…I don't know…die or something.

YOUNG HAROLD. Fear of Nirvana. That's why we of The West stay away from it. Contentment isn't good for anyone. Discontent is what gives us a reason to get up in the morning. Always steer clear of what you truly want in this world, Karla, because you just might find it, God forbid.

(With that, he raises his glass to **KARLA**, *and downs the rest of his drink.)*

KARLA. This is no joke, goddamnit!

YOUNG HAROLD. I'm sorry.

KARLA. Just go to bed. You're a fucking drunk.

YOUNG HAROLD. If you insist, but if I find you down here for more than five minutes brooding, I'll be down in my chicken costume, dancing like an imbecile.

KARLA. You won't have to come down.

*(***HAROLD*** *heads up the stairs.)*

BILL. You said that was the last time you saw her alive.

(As **BILL** *narrates* **KARLA**'s *actions, she performs them.)*

BILL. After you passed out upstairs, she took the gun you kept…scribbled her note…and shot herself. That's what woke you. You came down the stairs and found her. Her tear-stained note was on your chair. "Forgive me, my love. It's all too much. It always was. I blame no one but myself. Think only of the good. Love, kisses, and tears – Karla"

(There is a long moment of silence, then:)

So what the hell was that?! Nothing you've told me tonight explains that woman. I mean, Christ, if I'm supposed to believe you, you have to account for her.

HAROLD. I can account for her…you've read the…it's all…

BILL. It's all what? Either your statement to the police is a lie or everything you've told me tonight is. Which is it? Come on, you're the one Karla called "Keeper of the Truth."

HAROLD. *(dazedly, lost in a fog)* I'll wear the title proudly, my lady.

BILL. Harold, I know this is hard for you to accept, but every word I wrote was motivated out of love for Karla. I was one of those people who she communicated with in the dark, like you said. My book came out the way it did because that's the trail you left for me to follow. If there's a different trail, you've got to tell me about it.

HAROLD. I can't…

BILL. Tell me and I'll do what you want. I'll be fair. *(a beat)* I'll stop those trucks.

HAROLD. What if you can't?

BILL. If I can't, then, I'll, I'll print an addendum setting the record straight. Even though it means public humiliation, I'll do that for her. Karla is who's important here. To both of us. The Truth about Karla. Your Truth.

HAROLD. My truth…

BILL. Tell me, Harold. You can trust me. I swear to God.

HAROLD. You know, Bill, I was never any good at the real emotional moments of my stories. Never could get the meat right. All the delicious gravy, but no meat. That's what everyone loved about my movies – they didn't have to use their teeth. *(a pause)* You're right. That story is not worthy of Karla.

BILL. What do you mean "story"? That's not how it happened?

HAROLD. *(a finger to his lips)* Shhhhhh. You came here tonight to listen to my grand joke. Have the decency to be quiet for the punch line.

(Just then, the clock tolls three o'clock in the morning.)

Scene Nine

*(Karlaboy. 1953. **KARLA**, sleeping, is wakened by the chimes. She spots **YOUNG HAROLD**, sitting beside a nearly empty bottle of scotch.)*

KARLA. Will you go to sleep, Harold? You're not solving anything by staring at that clock. *(a beat)* That bottle was full an hour ago – did you drink all that? *(No answer* *from* **HAROLD**.*)* Fine. I'm going back to sleep. This rug is more comfortable than you'd think.

YOUNG HAROLD. I'm going to kill myself.

KARLA. Will you stop?

YOUNG HAROLD. I mean it.

KARLA. *(back to sleep)* Fine. Good.

YOUNG HAROLD. You think I'm joking?

KARLA. No. I think you're melodramatic.

YOUNG HAROLD. You don't think I'm capable of taking a gun and shooting myself?

KARLA. Go to sleep, Harold.

YOUNG HAROLD. Nothing goes wrong for you, does it? Nothing disappoints. You'll just walk in there tomorrow night and be handed that award.

(She sits up, starting to get pissed off.)

KARLA. I wish I wasn't even up for that damn thing! If I knew it would bring out this response – this asinine, petty ego thing – I would have been the first person in history to decline the nomination!

YOUNG HAROLD. Ego?! That fucking statue is not some game to me, Karla. It's not just five names on a ballot and fingers crossed. It means that somewhere in this pathetic life – this pathetic lie – somewhere in this make-believe art I kid myself I'm performing, somewhere in this sewer, I can come out on top. I can float. In spite of the compromises, the humiliations, the repressed passions that I cannot express on that screen or in my life – I can win! Don't you see?!

KARLA. *(gently)* Harold, no one thing should ever – or could ever – be all that.

YOUNG HAROLD. Look at you. Just lying there. Unaffected by it all, by everyone, by your nearing mythological hold on the American public. Hell, why limit it to America. Let's not forget about the Arab Sheik who named you in his suicide note or the British Duke who invited you to share his forty million dollar estate! *(a pause)* Tomorrow night you will be holding this…thing that would – yes – finally lend balance to my life, and to you it means nothing. How did you once put it? "I never expected this to go anywhere."

KARLA. Can't you be happy for me if I do win? Can't you ever just see me without all your shit getting in the way?

YOUNG HAROLD. All my shit...

(**HAROLD** *reaches into the drawer of the end table beside him and pulls out a gun.*)

YOUNG HAROLD. Does this look like I'm bluffing?

KARLA. How did that get down here?

YOUNG HAROLD. I brought it down when you curled up so peacefully and quietly and happily. My, you're such a happy person, aren't you, Karla?

KARLA. Please, Harold, you're drunk and you don't –

YOUNG HAROLD. Wanted to be a sexy actress – you're a sexy actress. Wanted the world to love you – the world loves you. Wanted recognition for your work – and tomorrow that too will come. All of it completely without effort. Practically between yawns. What do you want that you don't have?

KARLA. Leave me alone.

YOUNG HAROLD. Come on – there must be something, dollface?

KARLA. Stop it!

YOUNG HAROLD. There's nothing, is there? You are everything you ever tried to be and have everything you wanted to have, and that's all wonderful, Karla. Yes, I'm very happy for you. But do you have to be flaunted in front of my eyes, every day and every night – a monument to self-satisfaction – while I live in this studio-owned prison, in a studio-owned life, married to a woman I could never possibly love!

(**KARLA** *stares at him. Taking in the enormity of what he has just said.*)

KARLA. I wonder, Harold. Do you say things some times just to hurt me? To see if you can push me so hard that I'll fall into that horrible place where you spend your time? That place filled with so many words that there's no room for life. (**HAROLD** *has no response.*) What does he want from me, I ask myself every day. Maybe he doesn't know just yet…maybe some day he will. But I'm no closer to the answer, Harold. Not the one I want to hear. If anything, I'm further away. Further than that first ridiculous night when I tried to kiss you. Are we any less ridiculous tonight? *(a pause)* Oh Harold…what are you so angry about all the time? *(Still no answer from* **HAROLD.***)* I can't take many more nights like this. But I do know that I want you by my side tomorrow night. To hug each other whether we win or lose. *(a pause)* Who am I kidding?… The only person you can express genuine emotion for, real sorrow or real joy…is you.

(She turns to leave, heading for the stairs.)

YOUNG HAROLD. Then how do you account for the terror I'm feeling right now at the thought of losing you?

*(***KARLA*** *thinks about this before answering.*)*

KARLA. Fear of an empty theatre.

(She continues to ascend the stairs.)

YOUNG HAROLD. Are you leaving me?

KARLA. Haven't you listened to me? Do you even have the capacity to listen? I said I'd only leave you when I fell in love with someone. Well, I fell in love a long time ago, Harold. So I guess it's time for me to go.

YOUNG HAROLD. Karla, if you leave, I don't know what I'll do.

*(***KARLA*** *looks at* **HAROLD***. Sees him totally vulnerable for the first time in a long while. She descends the stairs and goes to him, engulfing him in her arms as he sobs.)*

KARLA. *(torn between her love and her misery.)* It's all right…I'm here…you're not alone… We'll…figure something out…some day.

(She gently takes the gun from his grasp and lays it down on the floor beside them.)

KARLA. You'll never have to use this.

YOUNG HAROLD. I'd never have the courage to shoot myself. It was all for pathetic show. Pretty sad, eh? Besides, –

(He picks up the gun from the floor.)

YOUNG HAROLD. No bullets. See?

(He points it at her temple and pulls the trigger –)

(Blackout as a tremendous explosion sounds in the darkness.)

Scene Ten

*(Karlaboy. Present. **HAROLD** and **BILL** are as we last saw them. Silent. Unmoving.)*

BILL. So that's it.

HAROLD. Yes.

BILL. I mean, that's it. You killed her.

HAROLD. Yes. That's it.

BILL. But what about the suicide note?

HAROLD. I'd been signing her name better than she had for years and no one but she and I knew. You never saw a more pathetic sight than a drunken Harold Bachman, sitting next to the corpse of his wife, desperately completing her now legendary suicide note. Taking her fingers…putting her prints on the pen… the paper…the gun…And it all worked.

*(**HAROLD** picks up the phone and holds it out to **BILL**.)*

HAROLD. Now make your call.

*(**BILL** looks at the phone and backs away.)*

BILL. Listen, this is…a little…overwhelming, you know?

HAROLD. Call them, damn you! You've heard the truth!

Now what are you waiting for?!

BILL. I don't know! I didn't...I mean, I expected you to tell me...something...but I didn't expect this.

HAROLD. I see.

(**HAROLD** *places the phone back down on the table.*)

HAROLD. You mean you never really had it in your mind to call off those trucks, no matter what I told you.

BILL. I don't know what I thought.

HAROLD. I'll tell you what you thought. You wanted to be able to say that you were the only one to hear the story of "Boy Wonder Bachman" straight from the ass's mouth. You never had any intention of helping me!

BILL. Mr. Bachman, let's get serious now. This whole thing is much bigger than just me. There's the publisher, the bookstores, money that's been –

HAROLD. YOU LIAR! You sat there all night behind your feeble talent trying to figure out how to use my story to boost your sales. A second book! That extra "bit of info" that could push Karla's story from a Movie-of-the-Week to a goddamned Miniseries!

BILL. Oh no. Not me. You're not gonna do this to me, too.

HAROLD. I've done something to you??

BILL. You're not gonna make me the latest villain in Harold Bachman's bio.

HAROLD. Why you contemptible –

BILL. (*interrupting*) Come off it, Harold – your father, the head of the studio, Tony – even Karla herself, you bastard. Everyone but you, Harold.

HAROLD. (*calmly*) Are you going to stop that book...or not?

BILL. Why? Because Karla's ghost is gonna come-a-hauntin'? Listen to me carefully: Karla's ghost is not going to kill you tonight. I'll even stay with you until six twenty-two just to show you that –

HAROLD. Answer the question! Yes or no?!

BILL. No.

(Without hesitation, **HAROLD** *picks up Karla's Oscar off the mantle and smacks* **BILL** *with it in the back of the head. He goes down immediately. Unconscious.)*

HAROLD. Then I'll stop her myself!

*(***HAROLD*** begins to look around at his environs.)*

HAROLD. Karla! Karla, I've done all I can!...I've told him the truth!...He's your biographer, not me! He's the printer of lies! I've...finally told...the truth...

(Wracked with fear, **HAROLD** *falls to his knees, sobbing. After a few quiet moments, he looks up.*

*(***KARLA*** is standing a few steps above him.)*

HAROLD. What are you going to do?

(No response from **KARLA**.*)*

HAROLD. Karla, this isn't you. We cared for each other, don't you remember?

(Again, silence from **KARLA**, *though her gaze is unwavering.)*

HAROLD. Answer me, damn you!

(At that moment, both **KARLA** *and* **HAROLD** *withdraw a gun from their clothing and point it at* **HAROLD**'s *forehead.)*

HAROLD. I didn't know the gun was loaded! I didn't know they'd turn my lies to the police into a legend of lies! I didn't want to destroy your life – I wanted to destroy mine!...Oh God, if only I had found a way to...love you...to love anything. My world...my life...would have finally come together...It would have been...perfect.

(Both **HAROLD** *and* **KARLA** *lower their guns.* **HAROLD** *takes* **KARLA** *in a sweeping "movie-movie" embrace, dips her, and kisses her gloriously.)*

(Lush romantic music swells gloriously, right out of a 1950's melodrama. All around, Karlaboy lights up like a grand paradise, no longer the darkened, shadowy hermit's lair.)

(HAROLD and KARLA come out of the embrace, looking up at their surroundings.)

(From above, PEOPLE begin to descend the stairs.)

(First, the STUDIO BOSS.)

STUDIO BOSS. Harold, baby, I love ya! *(a hearty handshake)* Anything you want, kid. Say the word, and I'll green light a picture about my own asshole!

(The STUDIO BOSS descends the stairs and begins to grab drinks from the bar, as if they have been gathered for a party.)

(From above, TONY now appears, also taking HAROLD's hand.)

HAROLD. Tony?

TONY. I forgive you, Harold. You're a better man than I.

HAROLD. The old Gunga Din epitaph...thank you.

(TONY joins the others below as – SYDNEY BACHMAN appears next at the top of the stairs, looking as he did in the "Mr. Foster" pictures. He is decked out in whites, blacks, and greys, and sports white face make-up and grey hair. The effect is that he walked out of a black & white movie.)

HAROLD. Dad?

SYDNEY BACHMAN. We're even, kid! *(He takes HAROLD's hand.)* You made me so proud, you seven-times-a-son-of-a-bitch! If I was gonna croak after making a picture, it was worth it for one that you penned.

(SYDNEY BACHMAN embraces his son. From below, REPORTERS have assembled. The same ones who turned out for the ribbon-cutting on Karlaboy.)

REPORTER #1. Father and Son Success Story! What a headline!

REPORTER #2. Hug again, willya? It'll make a terrific shot.

(SYDNEY BACHMAN grabs HAROLD again. Several Flashbulbs pop.)

(**SYDNEY** *filters into the gathering.*)

HAROLD. Thank you. Thank you all!

(*The* **PARTY GUESTS** *pay attention to their host.*)

HAROLD. Karla and I are – (*He turns to her.*) Oh, God. She's smiling.

REPORTER #1. And you?

REPORTER #2. Yeah, how do you feel, Harold?

(**HAROLD** *is beaming. Holding* **KARLA** *securely at his side. He is practically in tears.*)

HAROLD. Perfect. I feel…perfect. Like I can, Christ, move on…finally move on.

REPORTER #1. (*scribbling furiously*) What a lead quote!

REPORTER #2. Now that it's all come together for you, give us an angle – tell us about "The New Harold Bachman."

REPORTER #1. Yeah! The readers eat up that stuff.

HAROLD. The new Harold Bachman…

REPORTER #2. Yeah, the man who can move forward.

REPORTER #1. The man who knows who he is and finally has what he wants.

HAROLD. The new Harold Bachman? The new Harold Bachman is a man who…no, that's not good…you want the new Harold Bachman. Just a second – (*a nervous laugh*) – questions like that aren't as easy as they… The New Harold Bachman is a man of truth, full of ideals, integrity, action –

REPORTER #1. What kind of truth?

REPORTER #2. What exactly are those ideals?

REPORTER #1. Were there ever any?

HAROLD. I am Harold Bachman. A unique man with a body and mind and soul! These all still exist. They've been hidden, stamped out, and controlled by people and circumstance –

REPORTER #2. Never by you, though.

HAROLD. You are The Dead! I am alive! I am Harold Bachman!

REPORTER #1. And you have your arm around a ghost.

(HAROLD turns to KARLA desperately.)

HAROLD. Karla? Tell them, Karla…Go ahead, tell them who I am. You knew. I've finally told them who you are, you have to do the same for me.

(KARLA's gaze is silent once again.)

HAROLD. Karla?…Don't you know?

(KARLA refuses to speak.)

HAROLD. Damn you! Lie for me! *(leaning in to her, speaking confidentially)* If you do, I'll tell you a secret: I am the empty theatre that I was so afraid of.

(A hyper-loud, surreal chime sounds signaling 3:15. The PARTY GUESTS have completely ceased their merry-making. Like KARLA, they are still. All have their attention focused on HAROLD.)

(KARLA once again raises her gun to HAROLD's forehead.)

(BILL awakens.)

BILL. Jesus Christ – put that down.

HAROLD. She won't listen to you.

BILL. There's no one there. It's just you, Harold. You and a gun. *(looking at his watch)* Harold, it's three-sixteen. You're alive. It's over now.

HAROLD. It's not over! As long as that book is coming out, it'll never end. Look at them!

BILL. Look at who?

(HAROLD indicates the PARTY GUESTS, which BILL cannot see.)

HAROLD. Them! All of them! They're all still here! Still calling me a liar. First about Karla and now about myself! They're still waiting. Waiting for something meaningful. I don't even have something ordinary!

BILL. You have your script! The one about the man struggling to keep his integrity.

HAROLD. It's not finished.

BILL. So tell…"them" you'll finish it.

HAROLD. I can't finish it!…The subject matter…Integrity… It's always been…foreign to me.

(**BILL** *has no response.*)

HAROLD. I'll tell you something, Bill. There is something worse…so much worse…than an endless struggle to preserve what you've got inside. And that's realizing you never had anything inside worth preserving. *(to* **KARLA***)* I am The Invisible Man, Karla…and I have seen my reflection.

(**HAROLD** *alone raises his gun to his forehead.* **KARLA**'*s gun remains at her side.*)

BILL. Harold!

(Blackout. A gunshot in the darkness.)

Scene Eleven

(Outside the front door of Karlaboy. The Present. **BILL** *alone.)*

BILL. Karla said she wanted a man who would fall in love with everything that was ugly about her. *(a pause)* Well I guess that's me. When you write about people who are dead, people who exist only in black and white or saturated Technicolor…or grainy pictures from the morgue, you can make certain rationales to yourself: they're something more than human…or more often, they're something less than human. But Mr. Bachman had the nerve to exist. To breath so close that I could feel his breath. To weep in front of me. And goddamnit, I never asked for that! *(a pause)* To hell with him! Why should I believe in Harold's ghosts? All I saw was Harold Bachman pointing a gun at his own head. And even if the ghosts were there – they're not my ghosts! I won't be intimidated by them…or by her.

(Lighting reveals the **BILL'S AGENT** *is talking to* **RE-PORTERS**.*)*

AGENT. …and Mr. Lauder's addendum will reveal, among other things, that it was Harold Bachman, not Karla, who took a gun in March of 1953 and ended his wife's misery.

(There are gasps from the crowd, murmurs. People are stunned at this bombshell.)

AGENT. We expect to release the addendum in time for the book's second printing.

*(***REPORTERS** *shout out questions on top of each other.)*

AGENT. Folks, I'm sorry, Mr. Lauder has been through quite an ordeal tonight. We'll have a full statement released later today, so –

(A question rises above the rest.)

REPORTER #1. Mr. Lauder, did you know that Harold Bachman was planning to take his own life tonight?

BILL. No. Of course not.

REPORTER #2. What has he been doing inside Karlaboy for all these decades?

*(***BILL** *ponders this. Maybe for the first time all night.)*

BILL. I really don't know.

REPORTER #1. Can you elaborate on your agent's statement that Bachman gave your book his blessing tonight and called it – quote – an act of great love and integrity – unquote.

*(***BILL** *has no response.)*

REPORTER #1. Mr. Lauder?

AGENT. Okay, folks, it's really been a long night for all of us. So if you'll just…

*(***REPORTERS** *try to shout questions. The* **AGENT** *tries to drag* **BILL** *along.)*

BILL. No! Wait a minute!

(BILL pulls away from the AGENT's grasp. The crowd quiets down, waiting for his statement.)

BILL. Harold Bachman did not call my book "an act of great love and integrity." He did not give my book his blessing. *(a pause)* And after talking with him...neither can I. My thesis is false. My book is...not the truth.

(There are murmurs from the crowd. Questions are shouted out once again.)

BILL. I'm sorry. I have nothing more to say.

(BILL heads into the darkness and finds himself right in front of – KARLA DAVEN. In that moment, all else freezes.)

(The sudden appearance of her – mere inches in front of him – knocks the wind out of BILL. He is frightened.)

(KARLA moves toward him. He stares at her fearfully.)

(She continues advancing, opening up her arms. BILL is frozen from both awe and terror.)

(KARLA is now upon him. With her open arms – KARLA gently embraces BILL.)

(He is shocked. Stiff in the embrace. She continues to hold him. All at once, BILL starts to cry tears of great release.)

(KARLA continues to hold BILL soothingly, maternally, stroking his head.)

(Lights fade.)

End of Play

PROP LIST

PRESET: The manuscript for Karla's biography, Bill's coat and briefcase, cigarette case, lighter, Karla's Oscar, bar with glasses and two to three bottles of alcohol, stacks of newspapers and Daily Variety's.

ACT I

Scene 1 – Movie Slate

Scene 2 – Bill's manuscript

Scene 3 – N/A

Scene 4, 5 – Bill's manuscript

Scene 6 – Bill's manuscript, cigarette case

Scene 7 – sports section of newspaper

Scene 8 – Super Mogul's phone, Bill's briefcase and coat

Scene 9 – drink glasses for guests, Handsome Man's Oscar statue

Scene 10 – stack of scripts

Scene 11 – N/A

Scene 12 – thick script for Harold's personal project, much thinner script for "Love Swing"

Scene 13 – Harold's drink, 8 x 10 photo (seen only from rear)

Scene 14 – stack of 8 x 10 black & white glossy photos of Karla, a black pen or marker; 8 x 10 black & white photo of Sydney Bachman.

Scene 15 – N/A

Scene 16 – copy of "Daily Variety"

Scene 17 – Envelope for Gowned Actress

Scene 18 – Harold's bottle of booze

ACT II

Scene 1 – microphones and pads for Reporters, prop scissors, ribbon

Scene 2 – Harold's drink

Scene 3 – N/A

Scene 4 – cigarette case, lighter

Scene 5 – N/A

Scene 6 – N/A

Scene 7 – N/A

Scene 8 – Harold's drink, gun retrieved from drawer, Karla's suicide note

Scene 9 – bottle of scotch, gun retrieved from drawer

Scene 10 – Karla's Oscar (NOTE: should be preset for entire play on a mantle and used by Handsome Man in I:9), Harold's gun, Karla's gun, cameras and notepads for Reporters.

Scene 11 – microphones, cameras, and pads for Reporters

Also by
Steven Peros...

The Cat's Meow

Full Length / Dramatic Comedy / 6m, 8f, Doubling is possible.

Based on the true story of a mysterious Hollywood death, *The Cat's Meow* offers a fascinating cross section of Jazz Era characters who intersect for one notorious weekend on board William Randolph Hearst's yacht in 1924. The play was adapted for film in 2002, with a screenplay by the author, directed by Peter Bogdanovich, and starring Kirsten Dunst, Eddie Izzard, and Edward Herrmann.

Weekend guests include: Charlie Chaplin, who has been carrying on with movie star Marion Davies, a secret known to Davies' paramour, the married – and much older – Hearst; and movie mogul Thomas Ince, who is hoping to revive his flagging fortunes by forming a partnership with Hearst. Playing with fire, Ince tries to convince Hearst that he can handle both Marion's movie career… and her private life as well.

During its 1997 Los Angeles premiere, audiences and critics were both entertained and moved by this darkly comic morality play, laced with clandestine romance, Hollywood excess, and steadily heating tensions, which erupt in a shocking act of violence.

"Hearst Yacht Mystery is *The Cat's Meow*…A stylish and sardonically funny expose of corrupt Tinseltown values."
-Los Angeles Times

"Recommended – Hands Down! Will have you on the edge of your seat."
-CBS Radio

"A terrific new drama." '
-Los Angeles Daily News

"Steven Peros' intriguing fictionalized speculation imagines the worst as everyone cavorts through an oceanic orgy of intrigue, seduction, infidelity, blackmail, booze, drugs, and murder."
-Daily Variety

Please visit our website **samuelfrench.com** for complete descriptions and licensing information